The Wishing Horse Rides Again

"Hmm," said the old man. "What would you wish for if you could wish for anything in the whole world? Money? Jewels? Land? Power? Beauty?"

"Certainly not! All I'd wish is that my poor grandad could be well again."

The old man turned to Albert. "We don't usually do things for free, do we? But on this occasion, what about making an exception?"

You can read even more about Albert, the wishing horse, in *The Wishing Horse*, by Malcolm Yorke!

He's also written *Class Four's Wild Week* and *Scarem's House*.

And here are some more WONDERFUL Young Hippo Magic stories!

My Friend's A Gris-Quok
Malorie Blackman

Fisherwitch
Susan Gates

Diggory and the Boa Conductor
The Little Pet Dragon
Philippa Gregory

The Magic Spell Book
Eric Johns

Broomstick Removals
Broomstick Services
Ann Jungman

The Cleaning Witch
Cecilia Lenagh

The Bad-Tempered Dragon
Joan Lennon

Hello Nellie and the Dragon
Elizabeth Lindsay

The Marmalade Pony
Linda Newbery

Mr Wellington Boots
Ann Ruffell

MALCOLM YORKE

The Wishing Horse Rides Again

Illustrated by Jan Lewis

For Jack and Molly Ashby

Scholastic Children's Books,
Commonwealth House, 1-19 New Oxford Street,
London WC1A 1NU, UK
a division of Scholastic Ltd
London ~ New York ~ Toronto ~ Sydney ~ Auckland
Mexico City ~ New Delhi ~ Hong Kong

Published in the UK by Scholastic Ltd, 1999

ISBN 0 590 19856 4

Typeset by Rowland Phototypesetting Ltd,
Bury St Edmunds, Suffolk
Printed by Cox & Wyman Ltd, Reading, Berks.

2 4 6 8 10 9 7 5 3

Chapter 1

Long ago and far away in another country, there was an old man and a horse. The horse pulled a battered cart which had a notice painted on the side saying:

They had just entered this country after having adventures elsewhere, and the old man said to the horse:

"This looks a very pleasant land, doesn't it, Albert?"

And Albert said, "Yeigh."

"Look, there are lovely orchards and flocks of sheep and goats, and a peaceful village or two in the distance. I'm afraid the people here may just be *so* happy they won't need to use our magic wishes to improve their lives. Perhaps we shan't get any customers at all."

And Albert said, "Neigh."

They travelled on through the sunlit fields until they heard, from behind a hedge, a voice complaining: ". . .and when I got out of bed I couldn't find my slippers and then I dropped a piece of jammy toast on the floor. Oh dear what a terrible morning! Then one of the eggs I bought from the grocer didn't taste right and all this sunshine is giving me a headache. What is the world coming to? Then on top of that one of the sheep got her head stuck in a bush and. . ."

The old man and Albert looked over the hedge and found a shepherd talking to his dog. The man called them to come round and join him in the shade of a tree to share his lunch, and they gladly accepted.

As they drank his water and ate his bread and cheese and apples the shepherd said, "A pity about these apples – last year's were much better – and the bread's dry and the cheese is hard and the water's warm . . . but such is life."

Then he noticed the sign on the cart. "Ah, I see that you grant wishes. Well, I've got a wish."

"Really?" said the old man. "And what's that?"

"You see this sheepdog? His name is Eric and he's my very best friend. I don't know why, but somehow other people seem to find me boring so I talk to him all day long and tell him all my troubles. He listens to everything I say, but of course he can't reply. What I wish is that he could talk back to me."

"Are you sure?" asked the old man.

"I certainly am," said the shepherd. "And I've got ninety-nine gold pieces hidden away." He went round the back of the tree in whose shade they were sitting, and dug away for about ten minutes, then came back with a muddy casket which contained his life's savings. "Here you are. Now I wish you would make my dog Eric talk."

So the old man went over to Albert and whispered in his ear.

And Albert said, "Neigh."

There was a flash of lightning and. . .

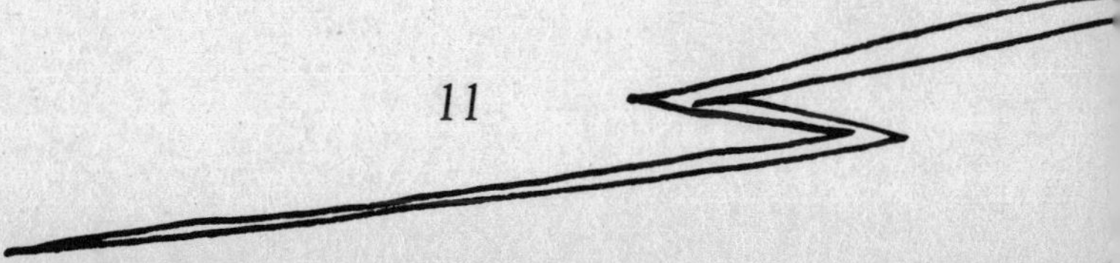

"At last!" said the dog in a growly voice. "Now I can get a word in and you can listen to MY problems for a change."

"Wonderful!" said the shepherd.

"Well, for a start I don't like being called Eric – it's a soppy name for a dog. And those biscuits I get are too dry so I need a lot more gravy on them, and then the blanket I sleep on is too rough and smelly, and since I work as hard as you do I don't see why I can't sleep on your soft bed with you, and another thing is I'm getting really fed up with chasing sheep, especially that daft ram called Gilbert, and what's more. . ."

The shepherd was so busy trying to get his reply in that he forgot to say thank you for the granting of his dearest wish.

"I think we'd better be on our way," said the old man, and he and Albert crept away down the road until they could no longer hear the dog growling out all his troubles to the shepherd.

"Do you think that was a success, Albert?" asked the old man.

And Albert said, "Neigh."

Chapter 2

They journeyed on until they came to a tiny cottage by the roadside. At the door was a very proud-looking lady who said, "Welcome, strangers. Of course, if life had been fair to me I would welcome you properly. My servants would offer you a drink and a rest and a bed for the night, but unfortunately, as it is I've only got one cup and one seat and one little bed."

And it was true. They could see that the one room of the cottage was entirely empty except for one cup, one stool and one bed.

"Well," said the old man, "Albert and I were about to stop to make a cup of tea, so why don't you join us instead?"

And Albert said, "Yeigh."

She consented to join them, and while they were drinking their tea, the lady saw the notice on the cart about magic wishes.

"I've got a wish I want granted.

Unfortunately, I don't have any money because I've always believed I'm too noble to have to work for it, but my neighbour has. I'll tell her to lend me some."

A little further along the road was another tiny cottage and the old man and Albert followed the proud lady to

its front door. She rapped loudly on the knocker. The woman who came to the door was obviously not rich either, but she welcomed them with a smile and asked them in. Her house was comfortable, and outside her tidy garden was full of fruit and vegetables. "Now how can I help you?" she asked.

The lady said in a haughty voice, "You've always said you wanted to be my friend, so now is your chance to prove it. I need ninety-nine gold pieces to buy a wish off this old man and his horse."

The neighbour looked rather surprised but said, "Of course I am your friend. As it happens, I have worked hard selling my vegetables and fruit, and I've saved up one hundred gold pieces to pay for my daughter's wedding. But you shall have ninety-nine of them if you think it will help you."

She went and fetched the money from its hiding place. Smiling, she placed it on the kitchen table before the lady, who snatched it up and gave it to the old man, saying, "Now grant my wish, and I shall live in the kind of grand style I really deserve. I always knew I wasn't meant to live in a one-roomed cottage, with people like this for neighbours." And she pointed to the woman who had just given up her savings.

"What is your wish?" asked the old man.

"I was born to be a great lady, so what I wish for is a huge palace with a hundred rooms and a hundred servants I can give orders to."

She paid over the neighbour's money, and the old man whispered in Albert's ear.

And Albert said, "Neigh."

There was a zap of lightning, and. . .

Instead of the proud lady's tiny cottage there appeared a colossal palace, ten floors high, each with ten rooms. Lined up at the gates were one hundred servants dressed in smart blue and gold uniforms. The lady strutted in through the gate with her nose in the air, ignoring the old man, Albert and her good neighbour. All the servants bowed to her and she immediately began to give a stream of orders.

"Prepare my meal! Order the carriage! Get me a new dress! Cut the lawns! Bring diamonds and pearls!" and finally, "Close the gates and keep those common people out!"

Then she disappeared inside, without a word of thanks or farewell.

The old man shook hands with the neighbour, who went sadly back to digging in her garden, then he packed up the tea cups and they resumed their journey.

"Do you think we did any good there, Albert?" asked the old man.

And Albert said, "Neigh."

Chapter 3

Further down the road they came alongside a golf course. They could see the flags, and the smooth greens, and the sand bunkers, with here and there pairs of golfers playing from hole to hole.

As they passed by a clump of bushes the old man and Albert heard a most tremendous smashing and crashing and thrashing and bashing, followed by a man's voice shouting the rudest words they had ever heard.

"Don't you listen, Albert; those words are unfit for a horse to hear," said the old man.

"Yeigh," said Albert, and put his hooves over his furry ears.

Suddenly, a white ball popped up out of the bushes, and after a few skips and bounces, it plopped into a deep pond and sank out of sight. Then a red-faced man emerged from the bushes, carrying a bag of golf clubs (mostly broken) and still swearing under his breath.

"Did you see where my ball went?" he demanded.

"Yes, it sank in that pond," replied the old man.

The golfer said a lot more very rude words, threw his club into the pond, then snatched off his golf hat and jumped up and down on it. "That's it! I'm finished with this stupid game!"

Then he tore up the card on which he had been keeping his score.

The old man sympathized, "So it looks as if you've not had a particularly successful day?"

"I NEVER have a successful day!" the golfer roared. Just then, his eye fell on the notice on the side of the cart. "You really make wishes come true?"

"Yes, we do," said the old man.

And Albert said, "Yeigh."

The golfer pulled out his purse, handed over ninety-nine gold pieces and said, "My wish is to be the perfect golfer. I want to beat everybody else and never lose."

The old man whispered in Albert's ear.

And Albert said, "Neigh."

There was a dazzle of lightning and. . .

The man put down a new golf ball, selected a club, and gave it a whack. It zoomed off through the air, and after one bounce disappeared down the hole in the far, far distance.

"Great!" said the man, and he put down another ball and did exactly the same again. Without a word of gratitude, he ran off, waving his clubs and whooping with delight.

"A satisfied customer, don't you think, Albert?" said the old man.

And Albert said, "Neigh."

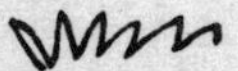

Chapter 4

A few days after this they came to a prosperous town, and in the middle of it they found a magnificent mansion. Obviously it belonged to a very rich family indeed. Lolling in a chair at the gate of this mansion was a very bored-looking boy. He was dressed in the most expensive clothes that money could buy.

"Hey, you!" said the boy rudely.

Albert and the old man came to a halt.

"I see you grant wishes. Well, you're going to grant my wish right now," said the boy. "In fact I'll buy fifty wishes, because ninety-nine gold pieces is nothing to me. My father's the wealthiest man in the whole country – so there."

"I'm sorry, but you can have just a single wish," replied the old man. "You see, Albert has only enough magic power in him to grant one wish at a time, then he has to have a rest to recharge his magic batteries. Isn't that right, Albert?"

And Albert said, "Yeigh."

"Stupid horse! Stupid old man!

Right, now let's get on with it." And the boy clicked his fingers for one of his servants to pay over the gold pieces. "I wish to own all the games in the world. Now! This minute!"

So the old man whispered in Albert's ear.

And Albert said, "Neigh."

There was a flare of lightning and. . .

Scattered all over the mansion's wide gardens there was everything you would need to play football or netball, tennis, chess, badminton, snooker, baseball, fencing, Monopoly, cricket,

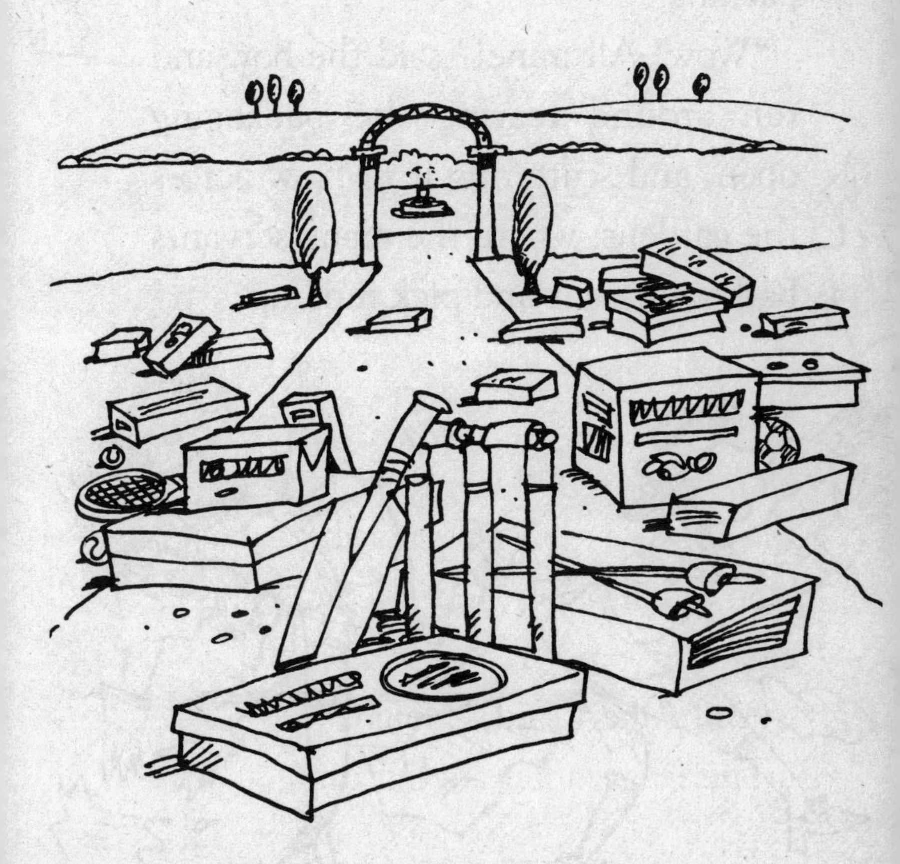

cards, draughts, basketball, table-tennis, darts, ice-hockey, snakes and ladders, boxing, billiards and a hundred other games. And all this equipment was brand new, still in its packing.

"Wow! All mine!" said the boy, and ran around tearing the packaging open, and scattering it to blow across the gardens, where the many servants had to chase it and pick it all up.

When he had opened about fifty packages a nasty suspicion suddenly came to him. "Here, you! Old man! I can't play any of these games on my own, can I?"

"No," said the old man. "You'll have to find somebody else to play them with you."

"Somebody else?"

"Yes, you know – share them, so you can both have some fun."

"Share? What's that? Share?" asked the boy, both puzzled and angry.

"I'm afraid we'll have to leave you to find out," said the old man, and he and Albert journeyed onwards, leaving the rich boy in a perfect rage.

Chapter 5

Some time later they came across a girl, running along the road and looking very unhappy indeed.

"Whatever is wrong?" the old man asked her.

"Oh, it's my grandfather – he's very ill. A tree fell on him in the forest and broke both his legs. He's in terrible pain. I've just run to fetch the doctor, but he refuses to come."

"Why not?"

"Because he says we haven't enough money to pay him, and it's true – we are very poor. Oh, I do wish I could help Grandad!" And she began to cry.

"Well, we grant wishes, don't we, Albert?" said the old man.

"Yeigh," said Albert.

The girl read the notice on the side of the cart. "But I haven't got ninety-nine gold pieces – all I have is the five pieces I offered the doctor."

"Hmm," said the old man. "What would you wish for if you could wish for anything in the whole world? Money? Jewels? Land? Power? Beauty?"

"Certainly not! All I'd wish is that my poor grandad could be well again."

The old man turned to Albert. "We don't usually do things for free, do we? But on this occasion, what about making an exception?"

"Yeigh, Yeigh," said Albert.

So the old man whispered in Albert's ear, there was a flicker of lightning and. . .

Round the bend in the road came an elderly man, but he was skipping and dancing and waving to the girl as he approached.

"Just look what's happened, my dear! I was in such pain, and then suddenly my legs were healed, and now they're stronger than they ever were!"

He gave a great leap in the air and twirled around like a ballet dancer.

"Oh, thank you! Thank you!" laughed the girl and gave the old man a hug and Albert a kiss on his hairy nose. Her grandad thanked them profusely too and the pair went skipping off, laughing, and hand in hand.

"Well, we didn't make any money – but I think we might have a satisfied customer there, Albert."

And Albert said, "Yeigh."

Chapter 6

By this time, many days had passed, and Albert and the old man had travelled right across the land. Before crossing the border in search of new customers in the next country, they decided to spend the night at a simple inn. After dinner, they were resting under a tree in the garden of the inn when they heard a growly voice, gradually getting louder and nearer:

"...and then that bone you gave me had hardly any meat on it, and anyway I never see *you* eating a scraggy bone – you just have the meat, and while we're about it, why do I always have water to drink? Why can't I have beer like you do? And another thing – that stupid ewe Emily is getting on my nerves, as well as..."

It was the shepherd and his talking dog.

"Please, oh, please," said the shepherd to the old man. "Will you shut this dog up! He's never stopped complaining since you granted my wish."

"Now you know what I had to put up with for years," growled the dog.

"I'll never complain again," promised the shepherd, "if only you'll take his voice away for ever."

"I wouldn't mind at all, so long as this old moaner's learnt his lesson," agreed the dog.

The old man turned to Albert. "A dissatisfied customer, Albert. Do you think this is a case for giving his money back?"

And Albert said, "Yeigh."

So the old man returned the gold pieces to the shepherd and whispered in Albert's ear.

There was a streak of lightning. . .

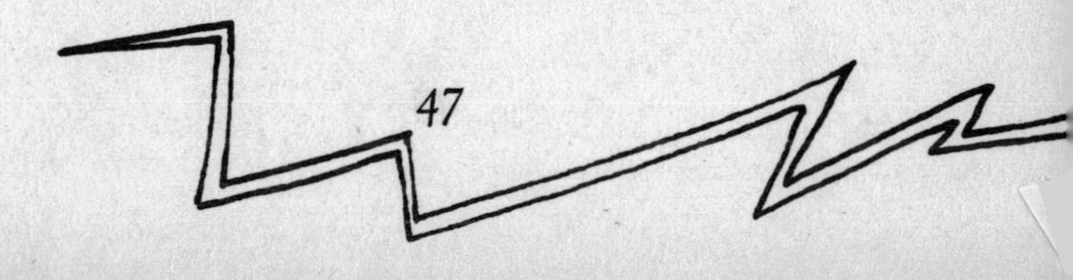

And the dog said, "Woof, woof."

The shepherd looked very relieved, expressed his thanks, and went on his way, the now silent (but tail-wagging) dog at his heels.

Soon after this, the lady who used to live in one tiny room appeared, looking very upset, and being comforted by the kind neighbour who had lent her the money for her wish.

"Oh, please make the hundred-room palace disappear and all the hundred servants with it," she wailed.

"Oh, deary me," said the old man. "Whatever went wrong?"

"Well, you gave me a hundred rooms all right, but they were all empty. All I had to put in them was one cup, one stool and one bed."

"But what about the servants?" asked the old man. "Couldn't you tell them to get you some extra furniture?"

"Somehow they didn't seem to like me ordering them around, and as soon as they saw how little I actually owned, they refused to do any work at all until they had been paid their wages. I didn't have any money. So they all walked out, and left me alone in my hundred empty rooms. I've never been so miserable in my life, and I want to go back to my little house again. It was simple, but it was mine and I could afford it."

"Oh, you poor thing," said her kind neighbour, giving her a hug.

"I'm sorry I've been so proud and rude to you before, dear, but I see now

you were my real and only friend." And she hugged the neighbour back.

"Another dissatisfied customer, Albert," said the old man. "Do you think she deserves her money back?"

And Albert said, "Neigh."

"Ah, yes, I was forgetting it wasn't her money, but her generous neighbour's." He then placed the money safely in the neighbour's hands.

The old man whispered in Albert's ear, there was a flare of lightning and. . .

Over the horizon, in the direction of the woman's home, there was a great rumble. The old man assured her that when she got back she would find that the hundred-room palace and the hundred servants had disappeared,

and that her own one-room little house would be where it had always been, and in it would be one cup, one stool and one bed. She was overjoyed, thanked them profusely, and set off home immediately, arm-in-arm with the one true friend she had. They decided they were going to work hard together at growing vegetables and fruit for the market.

Chapter 7

Soon after this, the golfer appeared, still carrying his golf bag – but now it only contained one club. He was looking very glum indeed.

"Well, are you still enjoying your game?" asked the old man.

"Oh, I play perfectly," the golfer admitted. "I win every game I play nowadays."

"So why are you looking so fed up?"

"Because every single time I hit the ball, it always goes in the hole. No matter which way I face, or what club I use, or what distance it is, I always get the ball down the hole in just one stroke."

"Always?" asked the old man.

"Always. I've tried hitting the ball with an umbrella, a spade, a stick of rhubarb, even with my friend's wooden leg. And every time I go round the whole eighteen holes in just eighteen strokes."

"But isn't that good?" asked the old man.

"It's *too* good, because nobody will play with me any more. And to be honest it's very boring being perfect and having nothing to improve on or practise. If you can't take my wish away I shall never play golf again!"

"Oh dear, Albert, another dissatisfied customer. Should we refund his money?"

And Albert said, "Yeigh."

The old man returned the ninety-nine gold pieces, and whispered in Albert's ear.

And Albert said, "Neigh."

There was a blaze of lightning and. . .

The golfer put down a golf ball, took out his one club, and missed it completely, four times in a row. Finally, he did hit the ball, but it smashed the window of the inn and he had to pay the furious landlord for its repair.

However, he was smiling (and swearing) again, and after shaking hands with the old man, and patting Albert in gratitude, he went off a happier man. Now he was no longer perfect, he was determined to practise his golf until he improved.

Soon a great gold limousine came thundering up, the door slammed open and the rich boy bounced out, red in the face with fury.

"Hey, you!" he shouted.

"Are you addressing Albert and me?" asked the old man, calmly.

"Yes, you! Remember all those stupid games you left me with?"

"The ones you wished for? Of course we remember."

"Well, I found I couldn't play any of them on my own. I needed to – what's that word you used? Share? *Share* them with one or more other kids."

"Yes," said the old man.

And Albert said, "Yeigh!"

"Well, I sent the servants out to round up fifty poor kids and bring 'em in, and I said things like, 'Hey, you! Play football with me this minute!' or 'Hey, you! Play dominoes with me, now!' And do you know what they all said?"

"No," said the old man.

And Albert said, "Neigh."

The boy stamped his foot. "Every single one of them said, 'Push off, you rude little brat.'"

The old man nodded. "And I'm going to say the same. Push off, you rude little brat."

And Albert said, "Yeigh. Yeigh."

"What!" The boy was absolutely purple in the face with rage, but there was nothing he could do about it. Nor did he get his money back.

The old man whispered in Albert's ear.

And Albert said, "Yeigh."

There was a zip of lightning and. . .

Back at the boy's mansion, all the games disappeared and reappeared on the back doorsteps of the fifty poor children whom the rich boy had ordered to play with him.

The rich boy got back into his limousine, looking thoughtful. Perhaps, he was thinking, he ought to try this sharing idea after all, and see if anyone would be his friend.

Finally, the girl and her grandfather reappeared, both smiling.

"We have come to say thank you once more," they both said. "We'd also like to give you a present for helping us, so here is a sack of oats and a bag of apples for Albert, and here are some of our home-made cheeses, butter and bread for you, sir."

The old man and Albert were very pleased with their gifts, and put them away in the cart to eat on their journey.

Then they crossed the border into the next land, where there were a few more people who still needed to learn how to say thank you, and to use their wishes properly.

The End